DESI
FOR
PRESIDENT

By
Cathy Rogers
and
Deborah Shlian

Copyright © 2020 by Cathy Rogers and Deborah Shlian

DESI FOR PRESIDENT

Published by Colony Publishing

Printed in the United States of America

Digital ISBN: 978-1-7346219-0-7
Print ISBN: 978-1-7346219-1-4

Cover Illustration/Design by Katie Stewart, Magic Owl Design

This is a work of fiction. Desi, Lucy, Cathy and Jeff are based on real dogs and people. Otherwise, name, characters, places, and incidents either are the product of the author's imagination or are used fictitiously, and any resemblance to actual persons, business establishments, events or locales is entirely coincidental.

All rights reserved. This book is licensed for your personal use only. No part of this work may be used, reproduced, stored in an information retrieval system, or transmitted in any form or by any means (electronic, mechanical, photocopying, recording, or otherwise) without prior written consent by the author. Any usage of the text, except for brief quotations embodied in critical articles or reviews, without the author's permission is a violation of copyright.

This book is dedicated to those who understand that only through kindness, honesty, and mutual respect can we truly achieve greatness.

"Kindness is a language which
the deaf can hear and the blind can see"

-Mark Twain

CHAPTER ONE

DOG ON A PLANE

"Sorry for the interruption, folks…"

The pilot's voice boomed over the intercom and my TV screen went blank.

"Just a little turbulence ahead. So buckle up."

Seated on Cathy's lap, I felt her comforting arms enfold me. "Don't worry Desi," she whispered in my ear. Not long ago, she and her husband Jeff had adopted me. My forever family. "Just a few bumps and then we'll have a smooth ride the rest of the way home to Los Angeles."

My friend Orville - he's a hummingbird- says I'm a lucky dog. He's absolutely right. How many humans get to fly first class? Let alone a one year old Poodle, Pomeranian,

Great Dame and Pit Bull mix rescued from an animal shelter. I am a very lucky pup. At home I have more than I could ever want- my own doggie bed, the best food, and toys of my own. For this flight Jeff had arranged my special treats. The stewardess brought it on a silver tray when she served dinner to the other passengers.

Now the pilot signed off and my TV screen illuminated the otherwise darkened cabin. Jeff said he was going to take a "cat-nap" Why not "dog-nap"? Lucy would know. Malamute shepherds are *so* smart. Wish she were here so I could ask. She was adopted from the same shelter many years ago. Unfortunately she's getting older now. The stoop in her shoulders makes traveling too difficult. So she's home with a nice lady who keeps her company while we're away.

Lots of "oo's" and "oh's" from passengers as the plane began to pitch and yaw.

I decided to focus on the TV to check my fear. On the screen was one shot and then another of mostly young people marching in the streets holding flags of countries I didn't recognize. In each, there were men rushing towards them, pointing guns.

Cathy must have sensed my interest because she turned up the sound.

"A decade that began with the Arab Spring is ending with street protests from Asia to South America and the Middle East," said the announcer. "With these violent clashes between police and citizens across the planet we can expect another difficult decade around the world. Who will be the next leader of America will mean the difference between war and peace."

Cathy, who is the most loving human I know, quickly changed the channel.

On the screen a group of humans were standing in a line in front of tall boxes. Some were raising their hands, others were pointing at each other, even shaking their fists. Most of them did not look happy.

"These men and women are running for President, Desi," Cathy said. "Each one is trying to convince the public that they're the best person to run our country."

Three moderators sitting at desks in front of the candidates asked lots of questions about how each would lead. However, instead of waiting for the person called on to finish his or her answer, someone on the stage would jump in, barking comments I thought were so unkind.

"He's a loser. Just look at his falling polls."

"She wants to open our borders to rapists and murderers."

"We don't need a weak person like him in the White House."

"Half of what you say is flat out false."

"Everything *you* say is a lie."

I was surprised to see humans who wanted the job of head of the United States to behave this way. The last person I heard yelling like this was the woman who first adopted me, then literally dumped me in the street. She was always calling me a bad dog even though I never meant to be bad. It was just that I was so hungry all the time."

After almost an hour, the debate ended and a panel of analysts came on. I was surprised that they all agreed with my feelings.

"The claws really came out, tonight," one of them said.

"Yes," replied another, "manners took a back seat as each candidate slammed their opponents."

"This was more like the hunger games- kill or be killed," a third analyst reflected.

"A giant food fight."

Cathy switched the channel to a station where a TV announcer was asking people on the street which candidate they thought won the debate. No one could agree.

Finally, the camera focused on an older man wearing a cap that read: Vietnam War Veteran. "Tell you the truth," he said, "I don't like anyone running. I'd rather vote for a dogcatcher."

That made me sit up in Cathy's lap. Was that even possible? A dogcatcher running for President of the United States?

I'd have to ask Lucy. But if it *was* possible, then why couldn't a dog run?

CHAPTER TWO

FOREVER FAMILY

These days it's wonderful to come home- especially to the beautiful house where I now live. It's in Malibu, California. Even though we live near the ocean, it's hard to walk there because the tides are so high. So sometimes we all go to the shopping center where I have gotten to know all the store workers who always give me a treat when I show up.

Other times, like today, Jeff takes Lucy and me to Legacy Park. It's really special. Lucy explained that years ago, the community decided to create an area to preserve nature. When it rains here, water is collected in a pond that is home to lots of different birds and ducks. Sometimes, I like to stop and watch the baby ducks swimming behind their mothers.

It's so cute the way they follow in a single line. For a second or two I do feel sad because I never knew my own mom, but then I realize how lucky I am to have Lucy as a big sister and Cathy and Jeff to love. And I have lots of dog friends that come here with their families. I especially like the little children who stop to pet me. I wag my tail like crazy then just to make them laugh. Isn't laughter one of the best sounds in the world?

Occasionally Orville even shows up, though I don't see him today.

There's a dirt path that surrounds the park. Unfortunately there are "NO RUNNING" rules here. All dogs must be on a leash.

Lucy says that that's because there are animals like poisonous snakes and coyotes that could hurt a pup like me. "Remember when you were running without a leash at the dog park in town and that nasty pit bull attacked you?"

I sure did. Still, it would be so much fun to try and chase the butterflies who land on the beautiful purple and yellow flowers along the path. I would never hurt them; I just like playing.

So whenever we're at Legacy Park, Lucy and I just walk side by side, sharing our thoughts. Mostly I listen to Lucy because she's so wise.

That's why I decided to tell her about the protests I saw on the plane's TV. "Lots of unhappy people in the world, Lucy. The announcer said the next leader of America will mean the difference between war and peace."

"I understand," she replied. "While you were away with Cathy and Jeff, I went on some walks with the lady who stayed with me. My dog friends said their families are talking about this next election for President. They're all worried about who might win. The problem is they don't agree and are starting to fight amongst themselves."

"I watched some of the debate on TV and was really surprised how mean the candidates were to each other."

"You sure they weren't just trying to prove they might be better than the other candidate?" Lucy asked.

"Well each did brag that he or she would be the best President, but mostly because they said the other candidates were stupid or liars. They actually used those words. Do you think a great leader should be unkind?"

"I certainly wouldn't vote for someone who was unkind," Lucy said. "That is, *if* I could vote."

I told her about the veteran who said he didn't like anyone running. "He said he'd rather vote for a dogcatcher."

"Let's hope *that* never happens."

"So a dogcatcher could run for President?"

"Sure, as long as he or she was born in the United States."

"*I* was born in New York. Does that count?"

Lucy made a high-pitched sound that I had learned was her laugh. "I'm pretty sure you have to be human to run."

"Pretty sure or absolutely sure?"

Lucy cocked her head and gave me a strange look.

"Just kidding," I said, deciding to hold off telling her my idea until I discussed it with a few more of my friends.

CHAPTER THREE

A VISIT TO THE VET

For the next few days, wherever I went, I made a point of asking the dogs I met what they thought about the upcoming election – at Legacy Park, at the mall, at the dog park, even at Lovi's deli where I always get a delicious cookie if I sit quietly in front of the selections in the glass case.

Every dog said that his or her family had been keeping up with the news – on TV, on the radio, on the Internet. That was good, I thought. It's important to know what's happening around you.

What troubled me was that they repeated what Lucy had told me: they were arguing with each other about who was the best candidate.

"What's terrible," one of them said," is tha family, they are taking sides. Everyone thinks th mother against father, daughter against parents, even grandparents are shouting at their grandchildren."

"They're just yelling at each other. No one is listening," another said. "My family is getting divorced over this."

"Oh my," was all I could think of as a reply. I couldn't imagine Jeff and Cathy divorcing. They were such loving people.

The more I thought about what was happening, the more upset I got. After all, the announcer on the TV on the plane had said that whoever became the next leader of America would mean the difference between war and peace. What then could be more important than picking a good leader?

When I am nervous, I start licking my toes. I couldn't stop. The more I licked, the more my toes started cracking and forming blisters. And they hurt. Cathy noticed right away and insisted on taking me to the vet that day. I was glad she let Lucy come too, just to keep me company.

Except for shots, which I definitely don't enjoy, I actually like Dr. Dean. He and his wife, Dr. Dana, who is also a vet, are really nice people. I especially like the receptionists. They all love animals - dogs, cats, rabbits, gerbils, even snakes. And no matter who is manning the desk, he or she always gives me a treat. And I do love treats!

The office is close enough from home that we can walk there. It's right next to Legacy Park. If dogs are staying overnight, the staff often walks them around the path before getting back to the dog hospital.

This morning there was a full house.

"Lots of anxious dogs," the receptionist told Cathy. "I don't know what's going on."

"I'll tell 'em," shouted a dog that looked like a pile of squishy wrinkles. She and her owner were sitting all by themselves across the room.

"Chinese Shar-Pei," whispered Lucy. "An ancient breed. Very territorial."

"What does that mean?"

"They like their space."

"So what's the reason there are so many anxious dogs?" I asked the Shar-Pei who said her name was Madame Ling.

"Some of the candidates running for President plan to let in too many mutts in our country."

"By mutts, you mean...?"

Madame Ling interrupted my question. "Dogs of doubtful pedigree." She held up her head in an obvious attempt to appear haughty, but the effect was lost by the way the skin of her neck was pushed together. It just resembled a stack of pancakes.

I would have laughed, but she was talking about dogs like me. *I'm* a mixed breed. I realized that some people would call *me* a mutt.

A beagle named Samson sniffed his disapproval (beagles are ruled by their noses). I had met him before and knew he'd once won Best in Show. He was always a good looking dog, but today he seemed as though he'd aged more than a few years. His eyes looked especially sad and his fur had lost its usual shine. "Don't speak for me, Madame. There's plenty of room in this country for all kinds of dogs – purebred like you and me and mixed breeds like my friend Desi here."

"You tell her," said Lucy who sidled up to give me a friendly nuzzle.

"I'll tell you why I'm anxious," Samson sniffed again. "My owner is so upset about this election that he's bought several guns. With so many angry people around, he thinks it's possible there may be a war in the future."

"I hope that doesn't happen," said Bennie. He's a Belgian Malinois who actually won a Purple Heart after being seriously injured during a third tour in Afghanistan. If there *is* a war, I know my owner won't hesitate to re-up and of course, that means I will too." The shorthaired shepherd was known to be loyal to a fault. He'd almost lost his hind leg after saving his owner pinned under an Army jeep struck by an IED. Lots of surgeries and months of rehab left him with only a minor limp. But I certainly understood his worry about having to answer the call to duty yet again. I couldn't forget that TV announcer. War or peace? We really did need the right leader as the next President.

"Desi!"

The nurse called my name before I had a chance to respond to Bennie. Lucy stayed with Jeff while Cathy brought me into the vet's office.

"What have we got here?" Dr. Dean asked as his assistant lifted me onto the exam table.

"Desi's been licking his toes again," Cathy explained. "It started a few days ago. The last time this happened was just after he came to live with us. Remember, you said it was because he was nervous about being in a new environment. I'm not sure what's worrying him now. We love Desi and he seems so happy with us."

Dr. Dean inspected the red blisters on my toes that I'd licked raw and shook his head. "I'm seeing a lot of nervous dogs these days." He lifted my chin and gave me a long look. "So what's bothering *you*, Desi?"

If he could have understood me, I'd have told him how worried I was about our country. But of course, only my animal friends could communicate. Instead, I made a little whimpering sound.

Cathy shrugged. "I suppose Jeff and I may have been paying a little more attention to Lucy since we got home from our vacation. She's getting older and we didn't feel she could make the trip. We wanted to make up for the weeks we'd been away from her." She sighed. "Guess I'll have to spend more time with Desi so he knows how much we care about him too."

"Sounds like a plan." The vet carefully wrapped my feet in gauze and tape. "That should keep you from licking those toes, my friend," he said, gently patting my head. He told Cathy to change the dressing every day. "Reapply the ointment and wrap it again until it's healed."

CHAPTER FOUR

FRIENDS & ENEMIES

I couldn't do much walking, let alone running, with my feet wrapped, so I spent the next few days in the backyard playing with a tennis ball. Sitting on the far side of the yard, Lucy pushed the ball back with her nose whenever I rolled it to her. Although I had been thinking about the election and what I'd heard from my dog friends, I wasn't ready to share an idea I'd been forming. I wanted to mull it over a little more first.

Today Lucy said she was too tired to play ball and was going inside for a nap. I was about to follow her when I heard my name called.

"Hey, Desi."

I looked up see a tiny green blur zipping in circles. "Orville!" My old friend, the hummingbird, was exactly who I needed to talk to.

"Just a sec," he said, then hovered over to the red feeder Jeff had hung from one of our trees and took a long sip of the sugar water inside. "Boy, I was thirsty," he declared when he was finished.

"So good to see you," I said. "It's been a while."

"I actually migrated here early this year. Because it's been warmer than usual, flowers like the ocotillo are blooming too soon. If I hadn't gotten to the desert this week, I'd have missed the delicious nectar I need." He did a few circles around my head, beating his wings so many times as only that tiny bird could. "It's affecting my hummingbird friends from west Texas to the Coachella Valley. They depend on the ocotillo. It's the only reliable energy source to complete their journey west . Not everyone has friends like you with backyard feeders."

"It *has* been really hot around lately," I said. "I heard Cathy say it's the climate changing."

"Exactly. Rising temperatures threaten the source of food for all 300 species of hummingbirds."

"That's really scary, Orville."

"Yeah, I just wish humans would do something. Imagine if they went to the grocery store and found no food. Worse, imagine if every grocery store within a day's drive was without food. So many seem to close their eyes to what's happening."

"If *I* were President, I would do something," I blurted.

Orville stopped in midair. "If *you* were President?"

"Do you think it's too crazy an idea for me to run?" I shared all that I had learned in the past few weeks – how the people were fighting with one another about the election, how no one seemed to be listening, how the candidates were too busy calling each other names to talk about how they'd solve problems like climate change. "Even my dog friends are nervous." I took a deep breath, realizing I'd been speaking without a pause. "You said it yourself, Orville. Someone has to do something."

The hummingbird made a few circles around me. "I was thinking more of some ONE like some human."

"Lucy said anyone born in the United States can run for President. *I* was born in the USA."

"You sure Lucy said a *dog* born in the USA can run?"

"Not exactly," I admitted. "But why not? I love this country as much as any human. And I have lots of good ideas about how to help people and animals."

"No doubt about the fact that are a dog of good character," Orville said. "I would vote for you. *If* I could vote," Orville said.

From under a nearby bush I heard a familiar voice. "Did I actually hear what I heard?"

"Is that you Sticks?"

The rat I'd met in New York before I found my forever family poked his snout out from under the leaves. "Thought I'd stop by to see how you were doing. What's this about you running for President?"

"It's just a thought right now."

"A pretty crazy thought." Sticks laughed and his whiskers twitched. "Even if you *could* run, you'd never win."

"Why not?" Orville asked.

"Desi's just a stupid dog. Ever since I met him, I could tell that he dreams too big."

"He dreamed about finding a family and look where he's living now," my hummingbird friend declared.

"I'll admit he's got a good gig right now, but nothing lasts forever. Take my advice, Desi – just go for walks and smell the flowers while you can. Stop worrying about this world. Like I told you way back when we first met: people are mean and selfish. I wouldn't be surprised if there is a war soon and everything ends."

"You were wrong then and you're wrong now!" I shouted, upset by his words. "Most people are kind and generous. They just need a new leader to help them see the way."

"And you think that's you?" Sticks' laugh was a nasty cackle. "I've got to get back to the sewer. But don't say I didn't warn you. You're setting yourself up for failure."

The minute he was gone, I looked up at Orville who was back at the feeder. "You think he's right?"

Orville finished sipping the nectar. "No, I had faith in you when you said you would find a forever family and I have faith that if you want to run for President, you can do that too."

CHAPTER FIVE

WHAT'S IMPORTANT

Orville's support for my plan gave me the courage to share it with Lucy.

After hearing me out, she shook her head. "It's nice that Orville stood up for you against Sticks, but you are a dog, Desi. I'm just not sure humans would ever welcome a dog as a candidate for the highest office in the country."

"Maybe that's because they've never had a dog like me who wanted to be President."

Lucy has a way of holding her head when she's thinking deep thoughts. I love that she listens to me and doesn't assume I am just a dumb pup. "Look," she said with an earnest tone, "if it *is* possible for you, a dog, to run for office, it won't be easy."

"I know," I replied, excited that Lucy was actually taking my idea seriously.

"You are going to need a platform."

"What's that?"

"Your message for the country."

"Hmm."

"Desi?" Jeff had come into the room. "Time for your follow-up appointment with Dr. Dean. Hopefully he'll remove the dressings for good."

I certainly hoped so. I missed walking and running.

"Lucy needs her rest. She'll stay with Cathy."

As I left the room with Jeff, Lucy called out. "Think about what's important to you, Desi. Then you'll have your platform."

All day long I considered what was important to me.

After Dr. Dean removed my dressings and in a stern voice, advised me never to lick my toes again, I realized how important being able to walk and run was to me.

On the way home, Jeff stopped at Lovi's deli and the nice lady at the cash register gave me two cookies because I was so well behaved. That's it, I thought. Food. Food is certainly important to me. My first owner threw me out on the side of the road just because I made a little mistake while she was driving. On the street I had to fend for anything to eat and when I did, I had to protect it with my life. Now that I have a new home and a forever family, I have more than enough to eat.

Before Cathy and Jeff rescued me, I was not only incredibly hungry, but lonely too. Now I have Orville and Lucy to keep me company. So having friends is important to me.

That night I was sitting on Cathy's lap while she watched TV. Lucy was curled up on the rug at her feet, softly snoring. Lucy's getting older now and needs more rest. I had my eyes closed, thinking about my conversations with Orville and Sticks and Lucy when something I heard made my floppy ears perk up.

"Rabbits taught me the true value of kindness."

"Rabbits and kindness?"

I opened my eyes to check out the TV screen. A pretty lady in a yellow dress was talking. She explained that she was a doctor who had read about a heart health study that fed groups of rabbits a high fat diet.

"You would expect every group to show the same results," she said. "But in fact, one of the groups had a much better outcome than the others."

How could that be, I wondered.

"What was different for the group that did better was that the researcher taking care of the rabbits was loving them. She would pick them up, rub their fur, talk to them. Her kindness protected those rabbits from disease." The doctor stared straight at the audience, "Can you think of someone who has shown you kindness?"

Of course. I thought about everyone in my life right now -Cathy (who was stroking my back just then) and Jeff who adopted me and gave me a wonderful new home; Lucy who's become my wise, big sister; Orville, who always believes in me; all my terrific dog friends.

"Their kindness makes us feel so good, right?"

Absolutely. I wagged my tail.

"What's happening in our homes, our schools, our communities these days is not okay. Bullying, shouting at each other, turning our backs on our neighbors- it's hurting our physical and mental health. Some people think it's a radical idea to be kind and show gratitude. But if we take care of one another, we will be healthier and happier.

Wow. I couldn't agree more. These days I felt as though everyone was judging without getting to know each other. We all come into this world different and unique. My father was a Pit Bull and my Mom was a Poodle. No human really wanted me until Jeff and Cathy. At the vet's a few months ago I met, Sheba, a new friend who had to have her front paw removed because she had cancer. Now whenever we see each other, we play together like nothing is the matter.

We are all the same deep down. Dogs feel it more except the pure breeds who are taught they are better. Otherwise we just love.

There is a lot of good out there as well as bad. I've seen both sides. Like I told Sticks: people just need help to see that way. A real leader. That's what's really important.

I jumped off Cathy's lap and thumped my tail to wake Lucy. "Didn't you say I'd need a platform if I want to run for President?"

Lucy yawned. "Yes."

"Well, I've got it now. What's most important to me is kindness, honesty, and mutual respect. That's going to be my platform."

Lucy didn't say a word, but from her smile, I could tell she approved.

CHAPTER SIX

GETTING THE WORD OUT

Now that Lucy was on board and I had a platform, I needed to get the word out. Lucy had an appointment at the vets the next day for her distemper shot (I'd already gotten mine, thank goodness) so while she was in with the doctor, I talked to Samson, Bennie and Madame Ling.

Samson, loved the idea of mutual respect. Even though he's a pure bred beagle, he understood that the world needs all kinds of animals and people, that diversity is what makes life interesting.

Bennie, who is a Belgian Malinois agreed that without honesty, there would never be peace and as a wounded veteran of the last war, he didn't want yet another.

Only Madame Ling was skeptical. But then I knew she was so unkind, she'd called me a mutt, said there were too many of us in the country. I had no intention of letting her selfishness spoil my commitment to a run for the Presidency – however crazy it might seem to some.

Every day after that, wherever we went, I'd stop to chat with any dog that happened by – at Legacy Park, at the mall, at the dog park. Most were really excited. "With all our families fighting among themselves, it will take a dog like you, Desi to show them the way to get along."

One day we stopped by Lovi's Deli. While I waited patiently by the glass counter for my treat, I heard my name being whispered from behind. I turned to see my friend Gracie, a beautiful mixed breed and a rescued dog like me. She lived a few houses away from Cathy and Jeff and we often met at the dog park. Today her owner's three-year-old daughter Beth had brought her in while she picked out a few cookies with her mother. Beth was one of these children with a beautiful laugh. I nuzzled her then so she'd look and see me wagging my tail. It worked. I got the best giggle from her. That made my day.

As soon as Beth's mother called her over to choose her cookies, I greeted Gracie with a welcoming yip. "Hi. What's up?"

"I heard you're running for President."

"That's right."

"I think it's great, but I wanted you to know I was at the park earlier today and a number of dogs- mostly pure breeds- are upset about your welcoming platform. They want you stopped."

"Why?"

"They like it when everyone is upset and unhappy. They're mean. Some of the bigger dogs like to take food from other dogs. The really big ones even eat little dogs."

That idea made me cringe. "Are you serious? Eat them?"

Gracie shook her head. "You are naïve, my friend. I'm telling you, these dogs bring their families out and get their babies to play with the little dog and then the pack comes and eats them. That's what they learn when they are young."

"I can't believe that."

"Believe what you want. I just wanted you to know that although most dogs are rallying for you, you should watch out for your enemies."

"Thanks for the warning."

"May I ask a question?"

"Sure."

"You've gotten the word out to plenty of dogs, but how are you going to alert humans? After all, they're the ones who will be voting."

To be honest, I had no plan, so I said nothing.

"I have an idea. My family feels the same way you do about the need for more kindness in the world."

I nodded. Everyone in Gracie's family were wonderful humans. They always had time to give me a gentle pat on the head or even a fantastic belly massage.

"My owner works for a local station. Maybe he can get you on TV."

"Wow, that would be amazing," I said. "There is one thing, though…"

"Here Desi." The lady behind the glass counter was bending over to hand me two treats. I barked my thanks, then turned to give one to Gracie.

Too late, she was hurrying out the door with Beth and her mother. I would have barked after them, but I didn't want to make a fuss. A Presidential candidate has to be well behaved. So I didn't have a chance to ask Gracie how the heck I could get on TV if I couldn't speak to humans.

CHAPTER SEVEN

ORVILLE HAS A PLAN

The next day I was sitting on the outside deck pondering this dilemma when Orville flew in for a visit. He was still searching for the biggest flower with the sweetest nectar. "So, Desi. I hear you really are running for President."

"I really am."

He flew in circles around my head. "So why don't you look happier?"

"I'm just worried. Yesterday I met my friend Gracie. She suggested that her owner could put me on TV. He works for a local station."

"But you don't speak human."

"Exactly." I lay down and put my paws over my head. I had no idea how to solve this problem. But without a way to let humans know I was running, I had no chance of winning the race.

A few more concentric circles and then Orville just remained in one spot, beating his wings hundreds of times a second as only a hummingbird can. "Wait, I have a thought."

I lifted my head to look at him.

"When I was visiting the Botanical Gardens in Griffith Park on my flower quest, I stopped by the LA Zoo next door. There I met an elephant named Netta who can actually write with her trunk."

"No way."

"Yes, it's true."

"You think she could be my voice? Make posters for me?"

"Maybe. I don't know why she wouldn't."

"That would be fantastic." I couldn't stop wagging my tail. The idea was really exciting.

"Okay." Orville began flying in circle around my head again. "Let me fly back and contact her. I'll return in a day or two."

CHAPTER EIGHT

SPIES

While Orville was away, I spent every waking moment thinking about my plans for my presidency and sharing them with more of my dog friends.

Lucy was especially helpful. She listened carefully to all my ideas, nodding when she approved – like equality for all dogs including mutts (like me), shaking her head when she thought I might be off the mark - like government guaranteed free treats (although she agreed that no dog should go hungry). Her suggestions that there be no kill shelters and serious fines for anyone who abused dogs were great additions to my platform.

Today the two of us were sitting on the deck, enjoying the California sunshine when Lucy said she was tired and was going inside to nap. My stomach was growling, so even though it was a little early for lunch, I figured I'd check to see if Cathy had left any treats in my bowl (which she often did).

I was about to follow Lucy, when I began to sniff the air. I may not be able to speak human but I do have a superior sense of smell, so despite the fact that he was concealed in the far bushes, Stick's distinct odor gave the rat away.

"Come on out, Sticks," I called.

Slowly, the big rat emerged. His expression told me he didn't expect to be caught.

"Why are you hiding?"

"Well, uh, I, uh…."

"Were you spying on me?"

"It wasn't me. It was Pullet."

"What do you mean?"

"I may have told him you had this crazy idea to run for President and he decided to find out exactly what you planned to do." Sticks mustered an embarrassed shrug. "I don't think he likes you very much."

I'd met Pullet at Legacy Park when I first came to live with Cathy and Jeff. He had beautiful thick red and white fur, a pink/brown nose and piercing yellow eyes. His arrogant manner made me assume he was pure bred, but Lucy said he was actually a cross between a coyote and Husky known as a coydog. "All the same, Desi, never tell *him* he's a mixed breed," she warned. "He has a temper."

Other dogs told me that Pullet liked to torture cats, but I was really surprised that he didn't like me. Whenever I saw him, I always made a point of saying "hi".

"Pullet has heard about your kindness platform and doesn't feel it fits in with the values of his dog pals."

"What would make him reject the idea of being kind to one another?"

"Terrible upbringing," said the rat.

"How's that?"

"I heard his first owner chained him up all day and beat him when he didn't obey."

"That's so sad."

"Now he hangs out with other dogs who were also mistreated. There's a whole group that's been meeting at the dog park. They're trying to figure a way to change your mind about running."

"How do they expect to do that?"

Sticks shrugged. "I have no clue, but then I don't get why you're running at all. You're a dog, not a human. Personally, I think you're nuts."

CHAPTER NINE

DON'T GIVE UP

I cannot lie.

The other day when Gracie told me to watch out for enemies, I hadn't taken her warning seriously. But Sticks' report today that fellow dogs were actually plotting against me was unnerving. His words really shook my confidence. I began to wonder if that rat wasn't right after all. Maybe it was ridiculous to think a mutt like me could actually run for the Presidency of the United States.

When I asked Lucy what I should do, she insisted the decision be mine and mine alone. "If you want to be the leader of this country, Desi, you can't be afraid to face your opponents. You have a great platform now. It's hard to believe anyone would argue with the idea of 'Kindness, Honesty, and Mutual Respect'."

I exhaled a deep sigh. "Yeah, except for Pullet and his friends."

"True," Lucy agreed. "Right now they plan to try and change your mind about running. But if you *really* want to be in this race, you're going to need to change *their* minds."

"You think I can do that?"

Lucy gave me a pointed look. "It's not what *I* think. It's what *you* think. I already told you, you have my support. Now you need to muster the courage to support yourself."

She closed her eyes and lay down with her head on folded paws, indicating that the pep talk was over, so I strolled outside to consider what she'd said.

"Hey, Desi"

I recognized the familiar greeting of my hummingbird friend Orville before I actually saw the tiny green blur diving by my head.

"Hey," I responded.

He must have recognized my less than happy tone, because he asked what was wrong.

I told him what I'd learned from Sticks about the opposition from Pullet and his dog pals. "I've been wondering if I should drop out of the race. Maybe it's just too much of a stretch to believe a mixed breed pup like me can make a difference in the world."

The hummingbird hovered in the air beside me. His tiny wings seemed to be beating faster than usual. "You couldn't be more wrong, Desi," he declared. "Remember, I was a little skeptical myself when you first told me about your plan. But after I listened to your words about kindness, I was convinced." He flew over to our red feeder and took a long sip of the sugar water before continuing. "I just flew back here from the Los Angeles zoo and I've got amazing news."

I sat up.

"Netta the elephant is so excited about your run for the Presidency. She's seen lots of human families at the zoo. She says that lately they are so busy fighting about the election, that they forget to enjoy the zoo animals. And they definitely don't enjoy each other. Their behavior has made Netta think that only with someone like you in charge, someone who will bring back kindness and respect for one another despite our differences, can we have world peace. She's in one hundred percent. And so are her animal friends at the zoo. So you can't back out now."

"Wow."

"She's going to do your posters and listen to this. Netta's friend Herman the anteater has agreed to talk to the Queen ant to help transport them."

I was amazed. With so much support from all these animals, how could I let them down. "Wait a minute," I said. "I have an idea. I saw a TV program where trees talk to each other. Maybe they can help get the word out."

"Talking trees? How do they do that?"

"According to scientists, trees share water and nutrients through underground fungal networks that they also use to communicate. They send distress signals about drought and disease, for example, or insect attacks, and other trees change their behavior when they receive these messages. Maybe they'd be willing to pass along my campaign message."

"Maybe," Orville said. "You really are smart, Desi. I never knew trees cooperated with other trees."

"Like I said, I learned it watching TV with Cathy and Jeff."

"Whatever, it's great that they get along so well. All animals should learn to live that way."

"We are one world after all."

"Maybe you feel that way, my friend, but a lot of others don't. And there seems to be more mistrust than ever."

"I know you're right, but we've got to work to make them see the need to change."

"So you're not going to drop out?"

I smiled at Orville, puffing up my chest with a new felt confidence. "No, I'm not. I'm going to do my best to win."

CHAPTER TEN

TESTING OUT THE PLATFORM

That afternoon, Cathy suggested we all walk to the dog park. She'd been spending more time with me lately – I think because Dr. Dean had misinterpreted my anxiety, assuming licking my toes was due to lack of attention. It wasn't true. I was worried about the state of the country, but I can't say I didn't love the extra scratches behind my ears or the wonderful belly rubs.

On the way I shared all the news from Orville with Lucy – how Netta was going to make posters and how Herman, the anteater had convinced his ant friends to help bring them from the LA zoo to Malibu. I also let Lucy know what Sticks had told me about Pullet and his gang.

Lucy gave me a pointed look. "And how do you plan to handle their opposition?"

"You made me see that I have to work to change their minds and that's what I plan to do."

"Good for you, Desi." Lucy's lips widened in her best smile. "And there's no time like the present to start doing just that."

"What do you mean?"

"I mean, that while we wait for the posters from Netta which will be for a human audience, why not test out your platform ideas at the dog park? It will give you a sense of how your message will be received. Today is Saturday. There should be more than the usual weekday numbers of dogs there. Mixed breeds, pure breeds. Big dogs, small dogs. I'll put the word out that you're going to be speaking."

I have to admit, I felt a little flutter of my heart as I thought about actually declaring my candidacy. But then I considered what Lucy had said about having the courage to support myself. So, I took a deep inhale, thinking *I can do this.*

Usually Lucy stayed on the leash even though unlike Legacy, this park allows dogs to run free. Today, however, she tugged her head so hard that Jeff finally got the idea that she wanted to walk around by herself. "Can't keep an old dog down, huh Lucy?" Jeff laughed as he unhooked the leash from her collar.

He took a seat on a bench next to Cathy. The two watched Lucy as she roamed the field, stopping to talk to every dog she met – Akitas, beagles, collies, terriers, spaniels, bichon frises, poodles, dachshunds, and plenty of mutts. One by one, the dogs trotted over to the far side of the park.

I waited until there were at least two dozen gathered there before I ran over.

"They're ready to hear what you have to say," declared Lucy.

Taking another deep breath, I began to speak. "Friends, I am officially declaring my bid to run for the President of the United States."

There were a number of cheers, but I have to be honest, there were boos as well. Still I continued. "I wanted to talk to you first before I made this announcement to humans."

"Talk to humans! How do you plan to do that? And a run for the Presidency? That's ridiculous. You're just a stupid dog. Dogs are pets and good for nothing else. Why don't you go back to the pound where you came from?"

I looked over to see who had made the ugly remarks and saw Pullet standing with a few of his pals.

"Why don't you hear what Desi has to say before you criticize?" demanded a service dog who I have to assume was insulted by the idea that his only worth was as a pet and nothing more. He knew the great job he and his fellow service dogs did in the world.

Pullet's ignorance was just the kind of talk that now inspired my commitment. "I can't deny that I am a dog. But maybe even more than humans, I understand the value of kindness. I also believe in always telling the truth. And I value the importance of appreciating our differences. So that's going to be my platform: 'Kindness, Honesty and Mutual Respect'."

This time the cheers clearly overpowered the boos, so I shared my ideas for a better world. I nodded to the group pointing out that yes, we were all different – some big, some small, some pure bred, some mixed. "But let's embrace these differences, not hate them. Let's all get along. Equality for all dogs."

An English bulldog named Hugo gave a positive yip. "Bloody good show, old boy." I knew the compact little powerhouse was intelligent, but I never expected his support.

The mutts barked their approval when I said that no dog should ever be killed just because rescue shelters were too full and that any human who abused an animal should be seriously fined.

"And no dog should go hungry," I added.

That was apparently too much for Pullet who snarled his disgust, turned and led his pals back to their owners.

Once they were gone there were no more boos, only words of encouragement so by the time Jeff whistled for Lucy and me to leave the park, I was feeling the happiest I'd felt since I found my forever family.

CHAPTER ELEVEN

A TEST FOR DESI

I guess I shouldn't have been surprised that the next day Pullet was waiting for me when Cathy let me outside to do my business. "Can I help you?" I asked.

"Actually," Pullet replied, "I'm here help *you*."

As hard as I tried, I couldn't keep the sarcasm from my tone. "Really?"

The coydog chose to ignore my skepticism. "Really."

I sighed. "Okay, I'm listening."

"My friends and I were very impressed by your speech yesterday."

"Gee, I didn't get that impression."

"Well, we had a little time to think about what you said. Especially about no dog going hungry."

Pullet's statement was so unexpected that I didn't know how to respond. Were Gracie and Sticks wrong about his being my enemy?

"I have something to offer you," the coydog declared. "A lifetime of dog biscuits. Whenever you like."

Now red flags went up. I certainly loved treats, but this didn't sound right. "Why would you do that?"

"I have a small favor, though."

"A favor?"

"If you become President, I hope you'd help get food for some of my pals who don't have nice families like yours."

"Of course I will do everything I can to see that every dog has enough to eat."

"My pals have special food needs."

"Which are?"

"Small dogs."

I wasn't sure I understood. "Huh?"

"Bichon puppies, toy poodles, teacup Yorkies. I'm not particular. They're all delicious."

I couldn't believe my ears. Even though Gracie had told me about this, I hadn't actually believed her. I guess Sticks was right. This abused dog had become an abuser himself. Apparently his friends were the same. I pulled myself up to my full height and went nose to nose with Pullet. "That's horrible."

Pullet lips pulled back over his sharp teeth in a sly looking smile. "It's a dog eat dog world, my friend. It really is."

"Not if I have anything to say about it. Get out of here. Now!"

Pullet shrugged and began trotting off. At the edge of the deck he turned and whispered, "Remember Desi, all the dog biscuits you want."

CHAPTER TWELVE

BIG SURPRISE

Several nights later Gracie's owner Margo was pounding on our back entrance.

Cathy, who had just removed one of the many cookies, cakes, and pies she'd baked for the weekend's Adopt-A-Dog event, shut the oven and slipped off her potholder. (I'd been hanging around while she cooked, hoping for a taste of at least one of her fantastic cookies.)

"Turn on the TV," our breathless neighbor shouted as soon as Cathy opened the door. "You won't believe what's happening."

Cathy switched on the kitchen television. "Which channel?"

"Right now it's on all the local stations, but it's only a matter of time before it goes national."

Jeff ran into the room. "What's all the commotion?"

Margo indicated the TV screen where Gayle Anderson, field reporter for KTLA was shaking her head. "Folks, just when you thought you'd seen everything, I'm not quite sure how to describe this scene on Pacific Coast Highway."

The camera panned a long line of what appeared to be a parade of large cardboard placards. It seemed to go on for at least a quarter mile.

"Are those moving by themselves?" Jeff wondered out loud.

Lucy sidled over to me. "Desi, I think that's…"

"Ants." I completed her thought just as the caravan turned off the highway and approached a familiar looking gatehouse. "Delivering my posters."

"Hey, that's our street," Cathy declared.

A helicopter hovered above the gatehouse, its spotlight illuminating the posters.

"Check out the words," Margo urged. "It's what I wanted you to see."

Jeff read as the helicopter camera dipped closer: "FROM NETTA AT THE LA ZOO; TO DESI IN MALIBU"

Cathy turned to me with a confused expression. "Our Desi?"

Jeff continued reading:
"MAKE HISTORY, DESI FOR PRESIDENT;
DESI FOR PEACE IN THE USA;
LOVE UNITES US, HATE DIVIDES US;
LET'S SEE THE BEST IN EACH OTHER;
LET'S SHOW WE CAN ALL GET ALONG;
FRIENDS MAKE THE WORLD;

FROM THE SEED OF LOVE, WE ARE ALL ONE HEART;
DOGS LOVE PEOPLE, PEOPLE SHOULD LOVE PEOPLE;
KINDNESS, HONESTY, RESPECT – DESI FOR PRESIDENT."

"Yes, folks," Gayle Anderson stated. "Your eyes don't deceive you. A parade of literally thousands of ants have transported these posters 35 miles- all the way from the LA Zoo to Malibu." She put her finger on her earpiece and nodded. "My producer tells me we're ready for Sam Rubin who is at the zoo now."

The picture switched to the entertainment reporter who stood beside a young man whose nametag said 'John Thomas, Animal Trainer'. "John, you just saw the ant parade in Malibu. Did you make those posters?"

"Not me. It was Netta."

"And who is Netta?"

I held my breath as the camera panned over to a pen where a large African elephant swayed back and forth like a dancer, her long trunk making loops in the air.

"She's beautiful," Lucy said and I agreed.

"Are you saying an elephant made those posters?" the reporter asked the trainer.

"I am. Netta is a real favorite at the zoo. She's well known around here for her ability to write and draw with her trunk."

"You're kidding."

"Usually it's a Happy Birthday or Get Well Soon poster, but this was obviously a special request."

"A special request from whom?"

"Well, I guess from Desi."

Cathy and Jeff turned to look at me. Now they both seemed bewildered.

Just then there was another knock at our back door. Margo's husband Lou had arrived with a cameraman and television crew. Gracie and Beth were with them.

Jeff opened the door to let them all in.

"I hoped you wouldn't mind," Lou said. "Margo called me when Beth's cartoon show was interrupted by Breaking News about the caravan. Once she saw it heading here and told me what the posters said, she guessed they were for your Desi."

Gracie's bark was more for clarification than agreement. She spoke to me. "It was Beth who figured the posters were for you. Kids are cooler than some adults."

As if on cue, Beth's laugher rang out, making me wag my tail for her.

"Anyway," Lou said. "I hustled over here with my crew for an exclusive. This is quite a story." He removed a mic from his bag and aimed it at Cathy and Jeff as the camera began rolling. "I know you've both been very supportive of the Adopt-a-Dog rescue program. In fact, you're preparing for a big event this weekend."

"True," Jeff said.

"So, is this a PR stunt to highlight your cause?"

"PR stunt?" Cathy asked.

"A dog running for president?"

There was laughter from the crew as if everyone agreed that the idea of my running was ridiculous. I wanted to hide in the other room with my tail between my legs, but Lucy nudged me to stay put. "Courage," she whispered.

"Tell us how you got the elephant to make those posters and the ants to carry them all the way from the zoo."

Cathy took a deep breath before addressing the unseen TV audience. "First of all, Jeff and I had no part in this." She pointed to me. "We knew that Desi was feeling anxious lately, but we assumed it was because I wasn't giving him enough attention. Apparently I was wrong."

"What do you mean?"

She leaned over to give my ear an affectionate scratch. "I think he's been upset about how we humans have been dealing with this election - families and friends fighting, no one really listening to one another."

"Desi doesn't talk. How did you get that idea?"

"Look at the words on these posters. 'Kindness, Honesty, Mutual Respect.' Can you think of a better message for our country in these divided times?"

"So you'd actually support your Desi for president?"

This time Cathy didn't hesitate. "Absolutely," she replied. "Like the poster says: Make History…"

"Desi for President," Jeff declared.

Gracie twirled in circles to show her pleasure, Lucy told me how proud she was and Little Beth clapped and laughed as I wagged my tail in delight.

CHAPTER THIRTEEN

DOGS CAN TALK!

There is nothing better than sitting in the front seat of Jeff's RV with my head out the window watching the world go by. I just love the wind pushing my face every which way. It's fun to bark at the animals I see on the side of the road-turtles, squirrels, even an occasional coyote. The only downside is that the wind dries my tongue and these days I need my best speaking voice.

Margo had been right. Lou's exclusive interview went national and then international. The phone started ringing that night and never stopped. Although a few people told Cathy and Jeff they were crazy to think a dog could run for the highest office in the land, most were excited about the idea.

The most interesting call came from the head of a software company that had developed a translator allowing humans to communicate in 60 languages. "I saw you all on TV and I'd like to help Desi speak." He explained that his engineers had been working on a way to translate animal sounds like barking into human words. "If you're willing, I'd love to have Desi be the first subject to test our technology."

Within a few weeks, I was able to bark a simple speech that highlighted my platform. Jeff hired a public relations firm to book me in every major city. Once the schedule was set, he and Cathy packed their camper and set out for what has been an exciting campaign tour.

I don't want to give the impression that the entire country is on board with a dog running for President. All the human candidates for that office got together and filed a lawsuit against me. Sticks is sure they will win the case. Orville and Lucy say 'you never know'.

So while I wait for the final verdict, I am having a great time, bringing my message of kindness, honesty and mutual respect to everyone who will listen. Here's what I say: "America is a great country. It's great because we are all different. We should respect those differences. We shouldn't hate or hurt one another because we are different." (That usually brings more applause than boos).

I finish my talk by explaining why I am running for President. "I just want to make this world a better place for future generations. So be kind. With kindness, honesty and mutual respect we can enjoy and build so much greatness together. Thank you."

THE END

A NOTE FROM THE AUTHORS

We hope you enjoyed this story. Desi is part Poodle, Pomeranian, Great Dame and Pit Bull. As a mixed breed, he appreciates that although all dogs are different, they deserve to be treated equal. After being mistreated by his first owner, he was rescued from an animal shelter. Now living with what he calls his "forever family", he understands the true meaning of kindness. He has a love for people and a desire to make the world a happier place. In this story Desi hopes to share this message.

All proceeds from sales of this book will ne donated to animal shelters and rescue organizations to help find homes for pets in need.

ABOUT THE AUTHORS

Cathy Rogers has taught culinary arts for thirty-five years at locations such as UCLA, on board cruise ships, at various cooking schools, and in private homes. She authored *Malibu's Cooking Again* to benefit the people who lost their homes in the Malibu fire. She is currently writing another cookbook. *Desi's Quest* was her first book in the Desi series, *Desi Needs A Job* is the second book in the series and now *Desi for President* is number three. Cathy hopes to use her books to inspire others and to give back to a world that has been so generous to her.

Deborah Shlian, MD, MBA practiced medicine in California where she also taught at UCLA. She has published nonfiction articles and books as well as 7 award winning medical mystery/thrillers. *Rabbit in the Moon*, an international thriller won the Gold Medal for Genre Fiction from the Florida Book Award. Shlian's newest stand-alone thriller, *Silent Survivor*, published in 2018, won First Place, Royal Palm Literary Award, was a Finalist for 2018 Best Books Award as well as Best Kindle eBooks; and won the Silver Medal, President's Award from the Florida Authors and Publishers Association. The third in her Sammy Greene series titled *Deep Waters* was released in November, 2019. Shlian's published novels are available in print, eBooks and Audiobook format. Revenues from sales of her books go to medical research as well healthcare organizations that deal with the issues in her books.

WOULD YOU DO US A FAVOR?

We hope you enjoyed reading *Desi for President* as much as we enjoyed writing it. If so, would you write an honest review of our book? Let us know if the story touched you in any special way.

Your review doesn't have to be long. Just a sentence or two will be great.

Your feedback is so appreciated.

Thanks so much for your kindness and generosity.

We look forward to hearing from you!

And, we hope you enjoy Books 1 and 2 in the Desi Adventure Series:

Desi's Quest and *Desi Needs a Job*

Available on Kindle and Amazon

Made in the USA
Columbia, SC
27 July 2020